Blushing Discovery

Tara Ijai

Deedra Abboud

Disclaimer and Terms of Use:

The Author and Publisher has strived to be as accurate and complete as possible in the creation of this book, notwithstanding the fact that she does not warrant or represent at any time that the contents within are accurate due to the rapidly changing nature of the Internet. While all attempts have been made to verify information provided in this publication, the Author and Publisher assume no responsibility for errors, omissions, or contrary interpretation of the subject matter herein. Any perceived slights of specific persons, peoples, or organizations are unintentional.

ISBN 978-1-956565-34-8

This book is dedicated to:

Love Rebels
on a journey of personal
discovery and growth.

May embracing your true self bring you joy!

Once upon a makeup mishap,
Tara found herself
lost in a sea of blush.

It was her daily routine,
like brushing teeth
or feeding her cat,
but there was a twist.

Every time she swiped on
that rosy powder,
instead of looking radiant,
she resembled
a tomato caught in a heatwave.

So there she was,
standing amidst the
makeup aisles of Sephora,
feeling more perplexed than
a squirrel in a maze.

Along came her friend Darian,
the makeup guru of their squad.

Tara, with a pout, confessed her
blush woes to Darian.

"What are you looking for?" Darian inquired with a quirk of her perfectly sculpted brow.

"Blush. But I can't find one that doesn't make me look like a clown," Tara replied with a sigh.

Darian's response was a
game-changer.

"Sure. But, just so you know,
I don't wear blush.
My face has enough red on its own."

And just like that,
Tara's world tilted on its axis.

She stood frozen,
her jaw threatening to kiss the floor.

The epiphany hit her like a ton of glittery eyeshadow palettes – she didn't have to wear blush!

Sure, some might say,
"Duh, Tara,"
but for her,
it was a revelation as mind-blowing
as finding out cold pizza
could be a breakfast food.

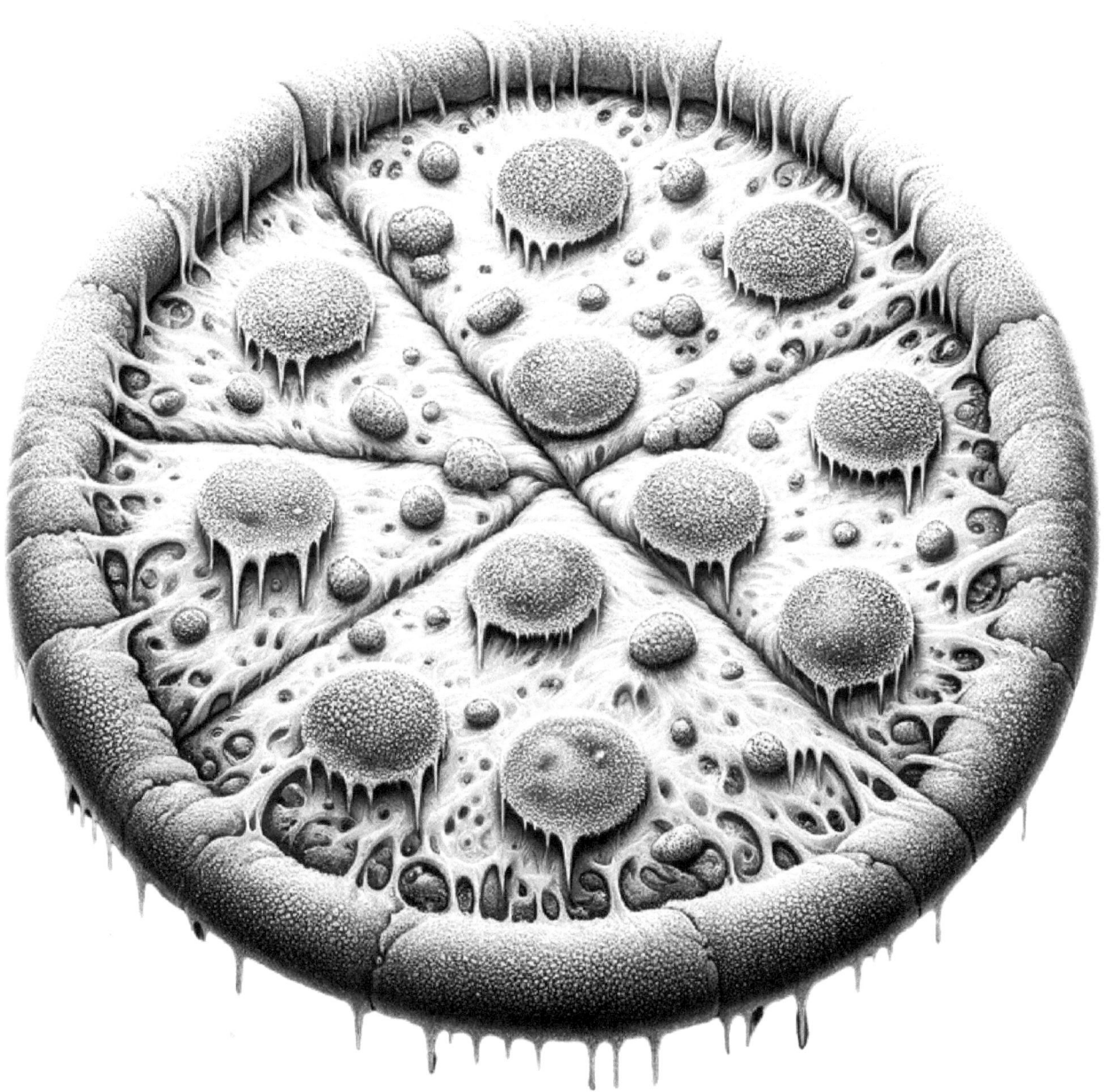

She realized she could question her routines, challenge the norms, and trust her own instincts.

So, armed with newfound wisdom
and a bare face,
Tara stepped out into the world.

No blush, no problem.

It was liberating,
like dancing in the rain
without a care in the world.

From that day forward,
Tara embraced her
natural rosy cheeks,
proudly strutting her stuff
without a speck of blush in sight.

She learned that living life
on her terms
meant listening to
her inner voice,
even if it meant
breaking a few beauty rules
along the way.

And as she walked into the sunset,
metaphorically speaking,
Tara couldn't help but feel like a
superstar in her own skin.

After all, life is too short to blend in
when you were born to stand out.

Check out other books in the *Tara's Life Unscripted* series:

@LoveGlassesRevolution